Britta Teckentrup

When I See
RED

PRESTEL

Munich · London · New York

I am furious.

I'm seeing RED.

I'm filled with rage.

A storm's ahead.

I'm blinded by fury.
I'm furiously mad.
But I can see clearly
that change is ahead!

I am
howling,
roaring,
whistling,
whirling.
Gushing,
pouring,
twisting,
twirling.

I am wild and
untamed.
I holler
and
roar.

I'm a
furious
dragon
you
cannot
ignore!

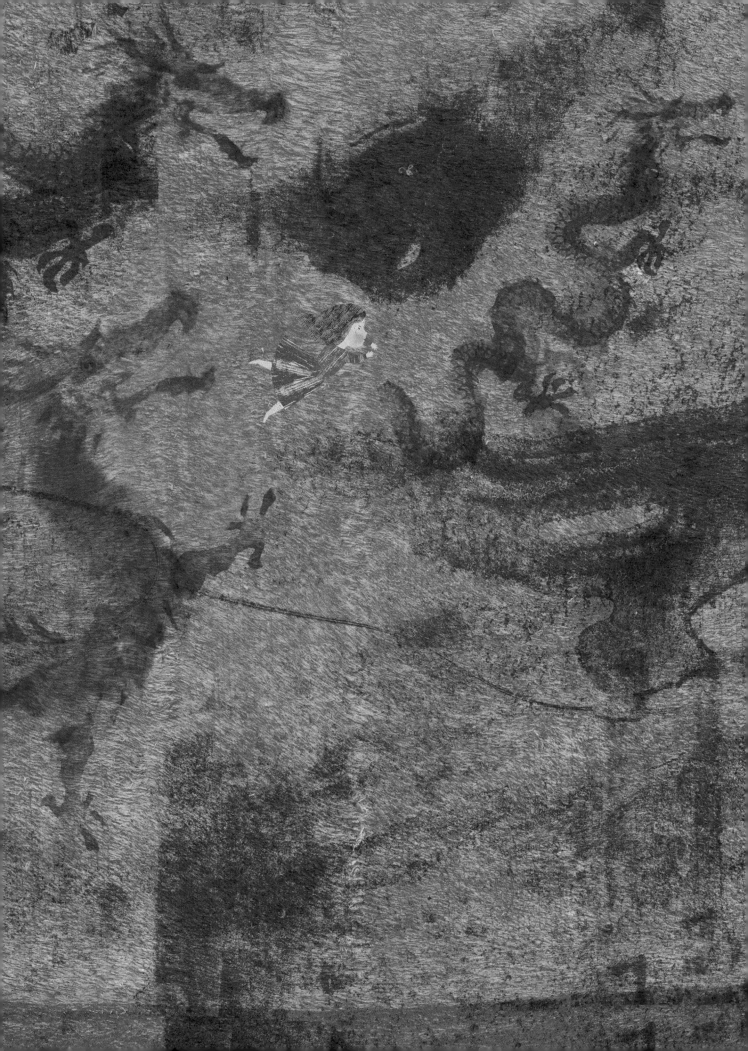

I am

hurricane,

whirlwind,

twister,

typhoon.

Thunderstorm,

lightning,

tornado,

monsoon.

I am
bellowing,
booming,
rumbling,
crashing.

Hurtling,
rolling
blazing,
flashing!

I do what I like.
I'm taking no orders.

I'm roaming the world,
     know no limits or borders!

I let it all out.
I roar at the sea.

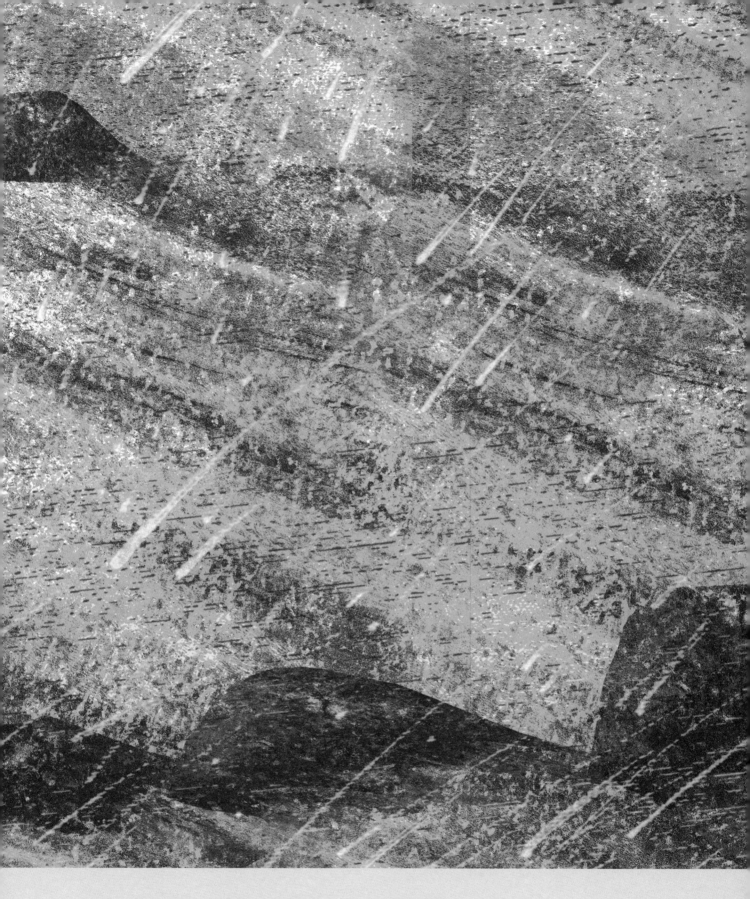

I'm flooding the shores.
Don't mess with me!

I'm riding the waves.
I'm in charge—watch out!
I stand strong, I stand tall.
I'm bold and I'm proud!

I am
flowing,
flooding,
surging,
slushing.

Streaming, swirling, brawling, crushing!

I'm calling forth monsters,
fearless and free.

Breathing fire and water,
I'm commanding the sea!

I didn't speak out.

I didn't know how.

I've been silent too long.

But look at me now!

My anger is loud.

My anger's a force.

It's the start of a journey
that leads to new shores.

My rage gives me power.

My rage keeps me safe.

My rage makes me stronger.
My rage makes me brave!

Rage pushes me forward.
I'm silent no more.

Rage unleashes a power
I cannot ignore.

Now I feel free. My anger has gone.

I take a deep breath. It's time to move on.

Everything is out. The air has cleared.

My monsters and dragons have disappeared.

The storm has blown over.

There's nothing to fear.

The door is wide open.

My journey starts here.

'Use your anger to transform the world around you.'

Anni Lanz (b. 1945), Swiss human rights activist with a focus on refugee policy

© 2021, Prestel Verlag, Munich · London · New York
A member of Penguin Random House Verlagsgruppe GmbH
Neumarkter Strasse 28 · 81673 Munich
© Illustrations, text and design: Britta Teckentrup

Library of Congress Control Number: 2021937969
A CIP catalogue record for this book is available from the British Library.

Editorial direction: Doris Kutschbach
Copyediting: Ayesha Wadhawan
Production management and typesetting: Susanne Hermann
Separations: Reproline Mediateam
Printing and binding: DZS Grafik d.o.o., Ljubljana
Paper: Amber Graphic

Prestel Publishing compensates the CO_2 emissions produced
from the making of this book by supporting a reforestation
project in Brazil. Find further information on the project here:
www.ClimatePartner.com/14044-1912-1001

Penguin Random House Verlagsgruppe FSC® N001967
Printed in Slovenia
ISBN 978-3-7913-7494-9

www.prestel.com